The Goodbye Boat

In memory of Grandad

Faith, hope, love

When you love someone and they love you, you are happy
together. When you have to say goodbye to someone you love,
you feel sad. When someone you love dies, you must say goodbye
for ever. At that time, you may feel that you will be sad for ever.

  This book is written to comfort you and to give you hope that
you will have happy days again.

  This book is also written in faith: that when someone dies and
is lost from our sight, they are just arriving on heaven's bright
shore.

  This book is written to remind you that the love that you
shared with someone is being kept safe in the everlasting love
of God.

Mary F. Joslin

The Goodbye Boat

Mary Joslin

Illustrated by Claire St Louis Little

Friends together

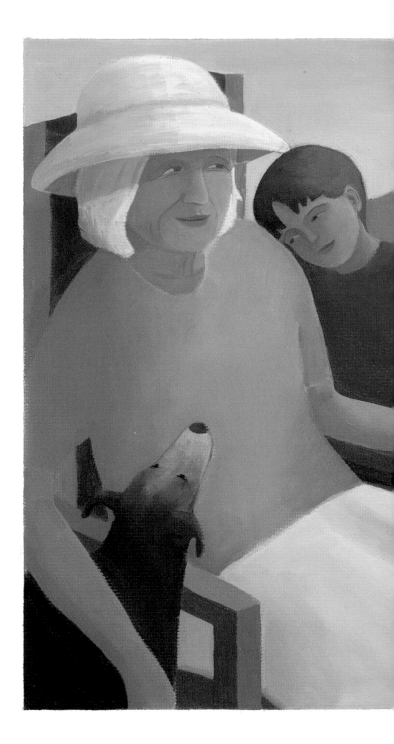

laughing,

loving.

Sad friends leaving,

wondering,

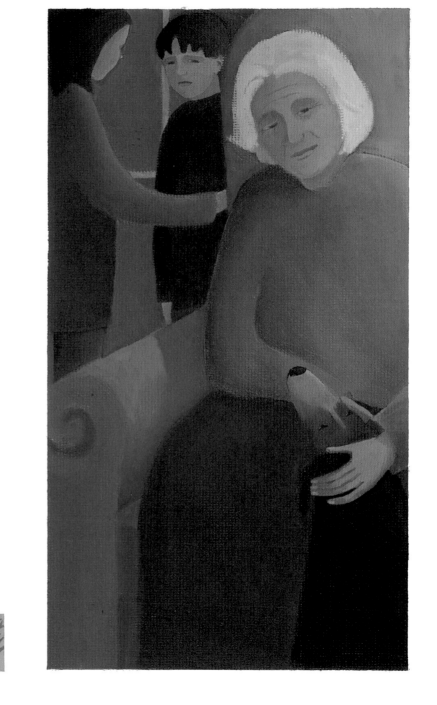

weeping.

Goodbye boat.

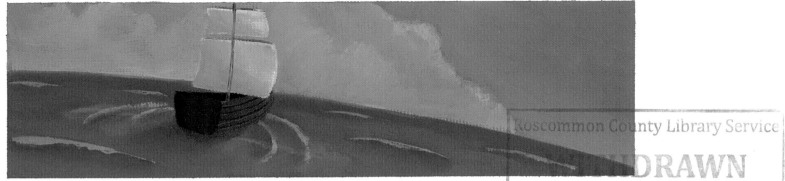

It's lost from sight.

 Lonely days,

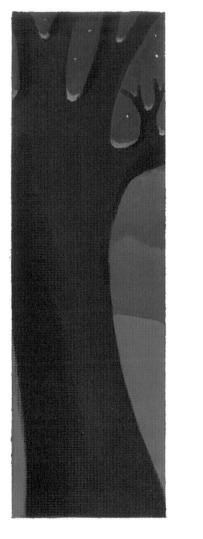

 a long, dark night.

Yet when the boat
has gone from view

it's surely sailing
somewhere new.

Mary Joslin is the mother of three children. When a much-loved grandfather of theirs died, she felt the need to find a way to talk with her children about saying goodbye for ever, and to provide a message of hope in the dark days of grieving. This book was written out of that experience.

Mary Joslin has written a number of other books for children, including *The Story of Easter, The Shore Beyond* and *Twilight Verses, Moonlight Rhymes.*

Claire St Louis Little studied at Falmouth College of Art. She is currently living and working in Oxford. ❧

Text by Mary Joslin
Illustrations copyright © 2005, 1998 Claire St Louis Little
This edition copyright © 2005 Lion Hudson

The moral rights of the author and illustrator
have been asserted

A Lion Children's Book
an imprint of
Lion Hudson plc
Mayfield House, 256 Banbury Road,
Oxford OX2 7DH, England
www.lionhudson.com
ISBN 0 7459 4264 4

First hardback edition 1998
First paperback edition 2005
10 9 8 7 6 5 4 3 2 1 0

Printed in Singapore

All Lion Children's Books are available from
your local bookshop, or can be ordered via
our website or from Marston Book Services.

For a free catalogue, showing the complete
list of titles available, please contact:

Customer Services,
Marston Book Services Ltd,
PO Box 269,
Abingdon,
Oxon
OX14 4YN

Tel: 01235 465500
Fax: 01235 465555

www.lionhudson.com